The Gummy Candy Counting Book

by Amy and Richard Hutchings
Photographs by Richard Hutchings

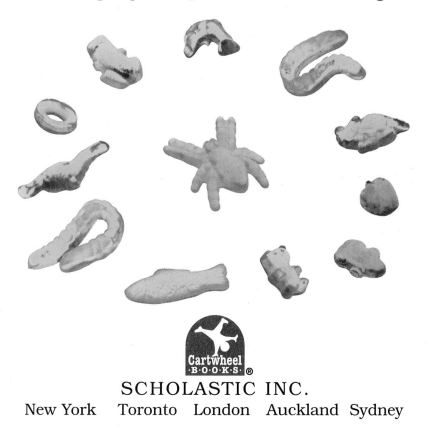

Cartwheel
·B·O·O·K·S·®

SCHOLASTIC INC.
New York   Toronto   London   Auckland   Sydney

*This book is dedicated to our mothers,
Molly Applebaum and Anne Hutchings, who taught us
how to count, and to our three delightful sons,
Jacob, Spencer, and Peter, who helped us test all the candy.
—R.H. & A.H.*

*The editors would like to thank
Dr. Stephen Krulik for his expertise.*

ISBN 0-590-34127-8

10   9   8

Printed in the U.S.A.   24
First printing, September 1997

Get ready to count
the things you love
to chew.
They come
in all colors —
red, yellow,
and blue.

Start right now.
This is going to be fun.
Count this gummy bear,
number
ONE.

1

Counting to
ONE
was easy to do.
Now try counting
up to
TWO.

1

2

This wobbly fruit
doesn't grow on a tree.
Count these
gummy strawberries.
There are THREE.

1   2   3

This is fun!
Now count some more.
These chewy dinosaurs
add up to
FOUR.

1

2

3

4

The worms
on this page
aren't
really alive.
But they
wiggle
and
jiggle.
Can you count
up to
FIVE?

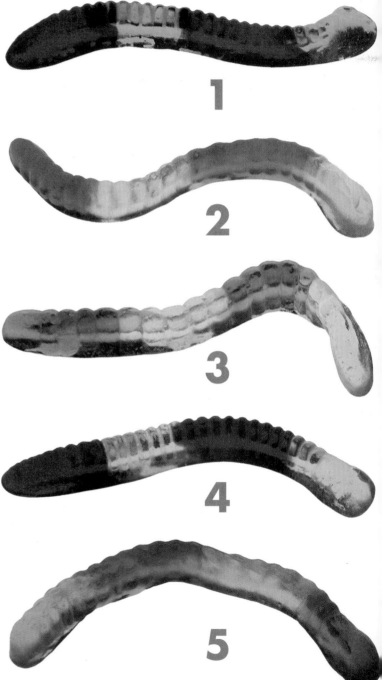

These fish
are so
yummy,
a colorful mix.
And they
like to
be eaten.
Here we have
SIX.

1

2

3

4

5

6

These big
juicy spiders
can give you
the *icks*.
To count
up to
SEVEN,
just add one
to six.

To catch
gummy fish,
gummy worms
are great
bait.
Count four worms
and four fish,
and you
will have
EIGHT.

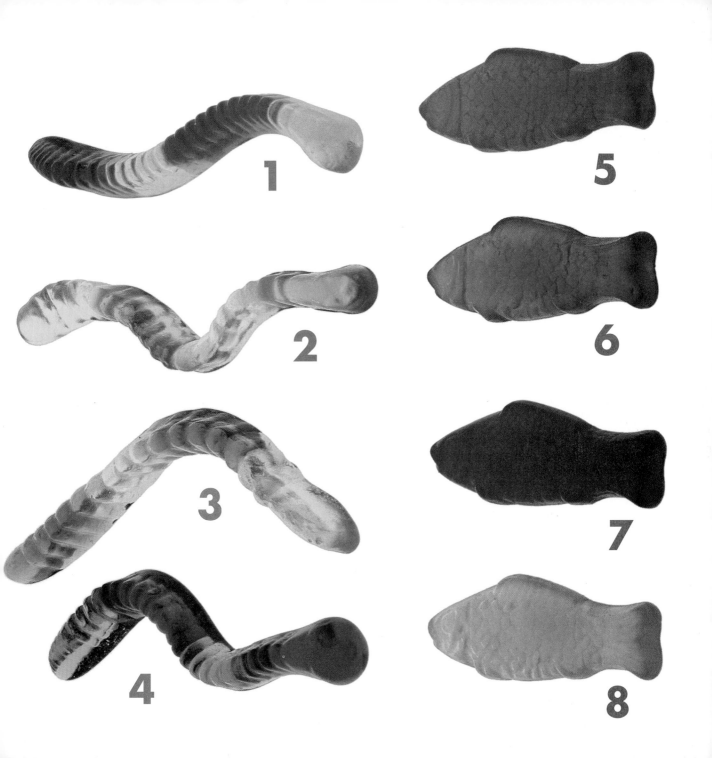

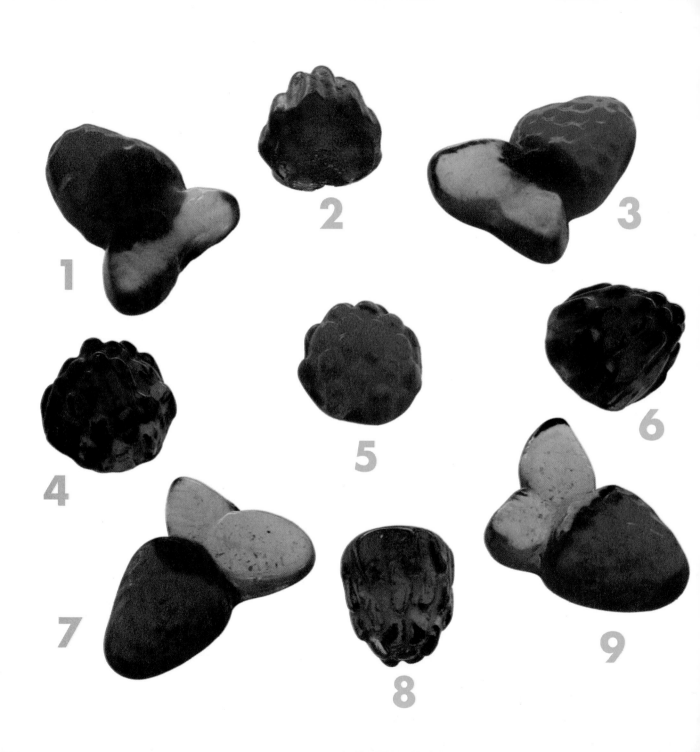

The berries
you see
make a juicy
design.
When you
count them all,
they add
up to NINE.

Red hot peppers
look so yummy.
But they can
burn your
mouth and tummy.
Count them
instead and you
will agree that
TEN
is the number
of peppers
you see.

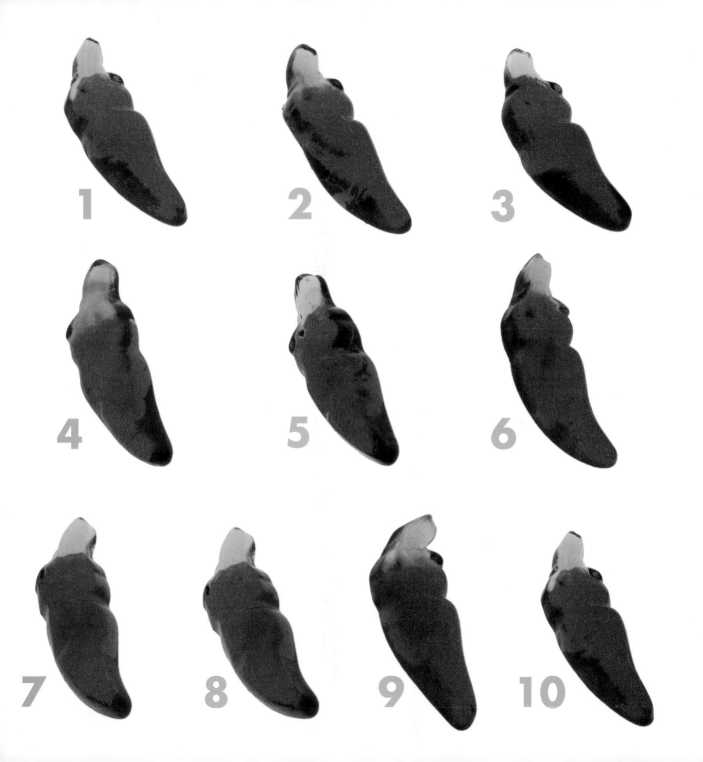

All the red candies
you've counted before.
You had a good time
and it wasn't a chore.
So look at this page
and count them again.
There are ELEVEN—
that's one added to ten.

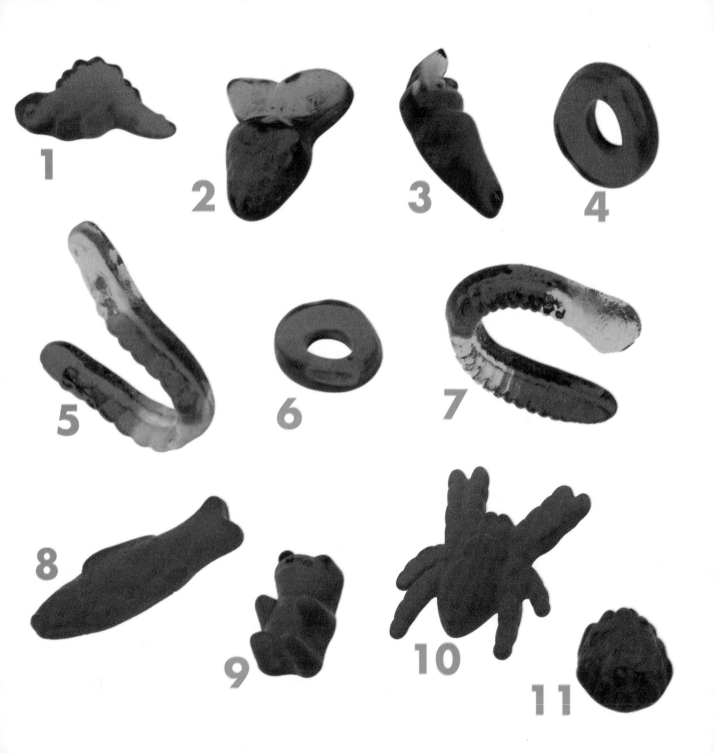

Did you count
to eleven?
Did you do it
yourself?
Now count
these blue gummies,
and you
will have
TWELVE.

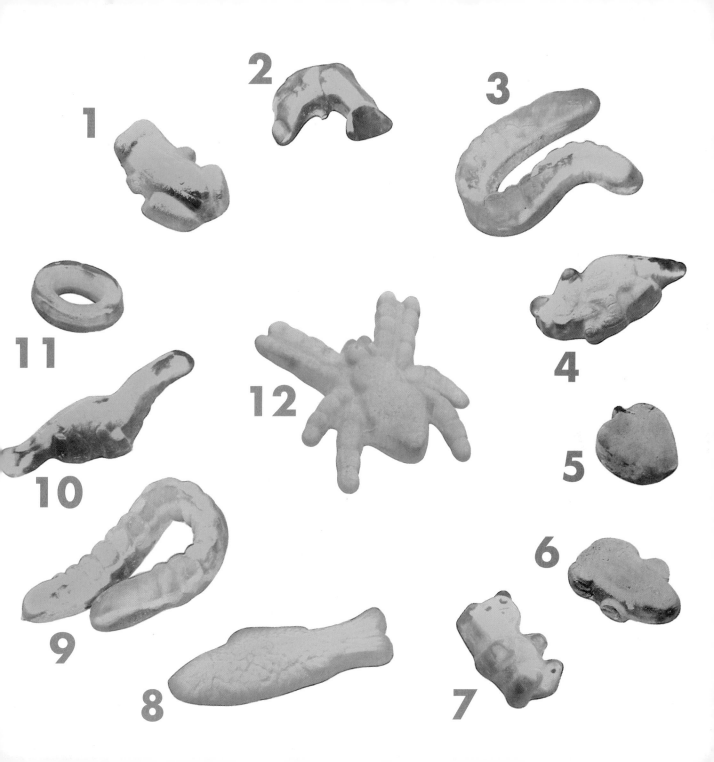

You've counted
to 12,
but you're
not finished
yet.
A group
of objects
is called a
SET.

Counting
ONE SET
of
12
is easy, you know.
Count all the fruits
lined up
here in a row.

1 2 3 4 5 6 7 8 9 10 11 12

TWO SETS of

6

are especially nice.

That's

12,

as you know, or

6

counted

twice.

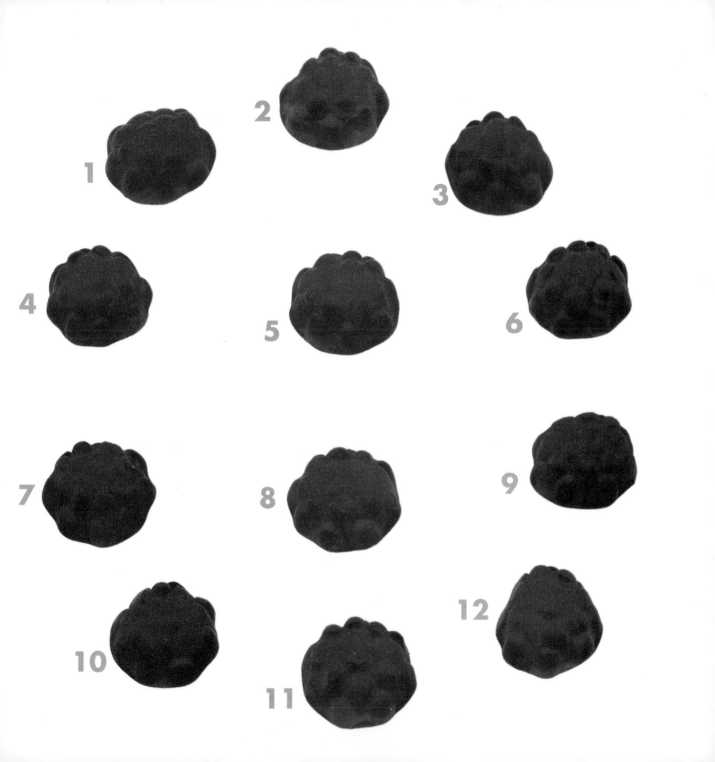

They all
look so yummy!
But wait —
there's more.
12
is also
THREE SETS
of
4.

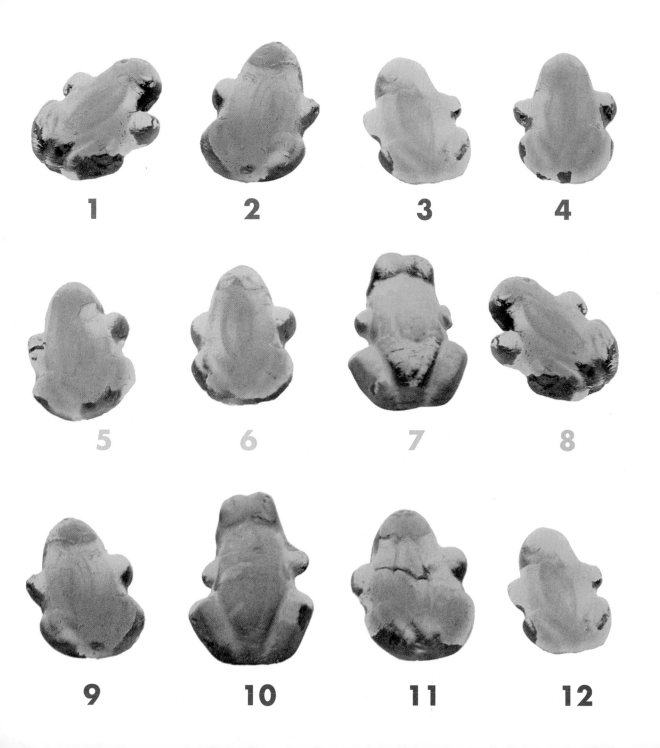

Dolphins are
mammals that
live in
the sea.
12
can also be
FOUR SETS
of
3.

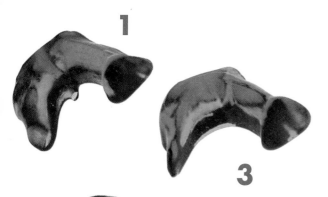

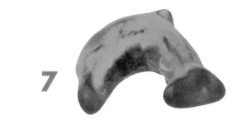
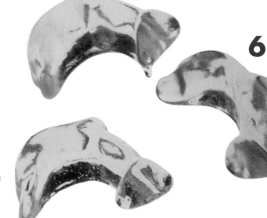
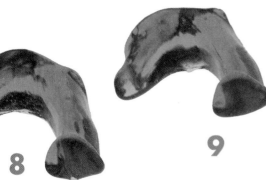
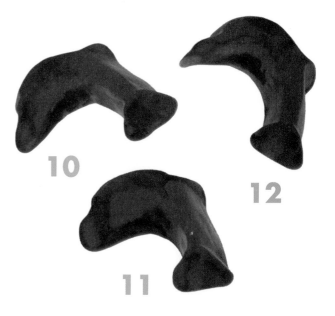

Count each cherry
you see,
and then
you are through.
12
of these cherries are
SIX SETS
of
2.

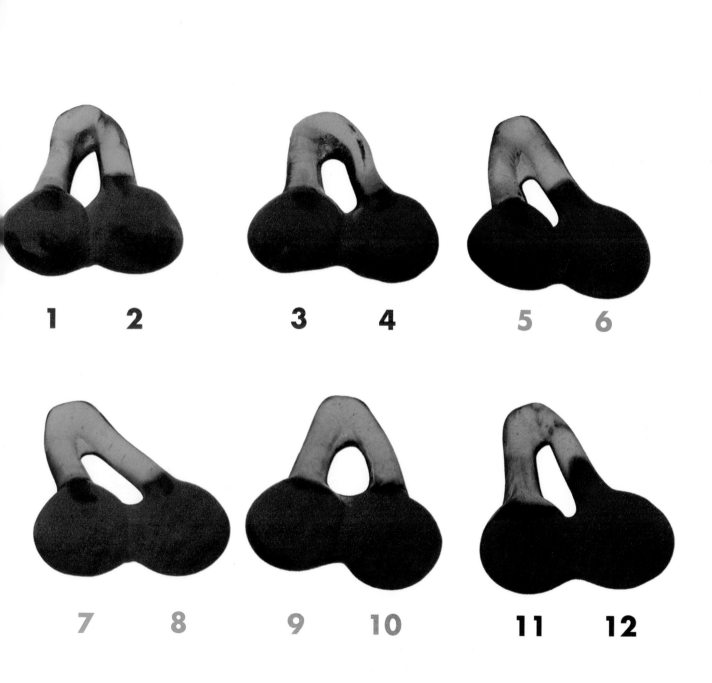

You should really
be proud
of what you have done.
You counted to
TWELVE
starting with
ONE.
You have
to agree
that counting is neat.
And now it's finally
time to eat!